How Anansi Got His Stories

Written by Trish Cooke

Illustrated by Anna Violet

OXFORD
UNIVERSITY PRESS

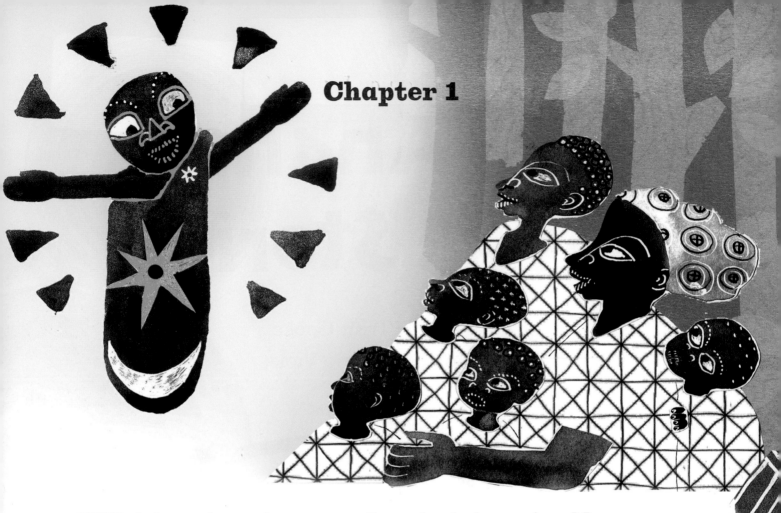

A long, long time ago, all stories belonged to Nyame, King of the Sky. All day long people would gather around him and listen to what he had to say. Anansi the spider was jealous of Nyame. He wanted people to come and listen to him instead.

"I want to own all stories," said Anansi. "I want to be King of Stories!"

"OK" said Nyame. "You can be King of Stories if you bring me the Hornets with their sting like fire, and Leopard with his big sharp teeth and Snake with his poisonous bite."

Anansi knew that the Hornets, Leopard and Snake were the most dangerous creatures in the forest and they would be difficult to catch, but Anansi wanted to be King of Stories so badly that he agreed.

"OK, I'll do it!" Anansi said.

Anansi was afraid. "How am I going to catch those three and bring them back to Nyame!" he thought. "I am not the strongest or the most fierce animal and I am not very brave…" he said to himself.

Chapter 2

 Anansi had an idea. "I will just have to use my skill, my wit and my cleverness to catch them out!" Anansi laughed and he went to fill a calabash with water. Then he made his way to the big tree where the Hornets live.

Anansi poured some of
the water from his calabash
over a big banana leaf
and he held the leaf over
his head to let some water
splash over him.

When he was dripping wet, Anansi climbed up the tree and sat above the Hornets' nest and poured some more water onto the big banana leaf. He let the water trickle down until it wet all of the Hornets in their nest.

"It's raining! It's raining!"
the Hornets cried.

"Come and take shelter in
my calabash!" shouted Anansi.
"It's nice and dry in there!"

The Hornets flew out of their
soaking nest at once …

... straight into Anansi's empty calabash.
When all of the Hornets were in Anansi's
calabash trap, Anansi quickly plugged
the hole with the banana leaf so that the
Hornets could not get out.

"Got you!" Anansi laughed.

Chapter 3

Anansi ran all the way back to see Nyame.

"I have them!" Anansi sang, "I have the Hornets! I used my skill to catch them. I deserve to be King of Stories."

"But you do not have Leopard or Snake," said Nyame. "So you cannot have my stories."

"Oh no," thought Anansi. "I had almost forgotten. I still have Leopard with his big sharp teeth and Snake with his poisonous bite to catch. What am I going to do? I am not the strongest or the most fierce and I am not very brave …" he said to himself.

Chapter 4

"I will just have to use more of my skill, my wit and my cleverness to catch them out!" Anansi chuckled.

Anansi went to get a big shovel and he found the tree where Leopard likes to take his afternoon nap.

Not too far away from Leopard, Anansi began to dig quietly. Anansi dug deeper and deeper until he had dug a great big hole. Then he covered the hole with grass and twigs and leaves.

13

When Leopard came out of the long grass to take his night time walk, he stepped on the hole covered with grass and twigs and leaves and ...

... THUD! Down he fell. Anansi began to spin a giant spider's web.

"Let me help you!" Anansi shouted down the hole. "Grab hold of my web and I'll pull you out!"

15

"Ah, thank you!" said Leopard and he grabbed hold of Anansi's web.

But Leopard got tangled in the web and when Anansi pulled him out of the hole, Leopard could not move.

"Got you!" Anansi laughed.

Chapter 5

"Let me go! Let me go!" Leopard roared.

"Let you go?" Anansi laughed. "Why would I do that when I have gone to so much trouble to catch you!"

"You wicked trickster!" roared Leopard. "I might have known it was you all along, Anansi!"

But Anansi did not care about Leopard's remarks. He was one step closer to gaining his crown!

Anansi dragged Leopard all the way back to Nyame.

"I have him!" Anansi sang. "I have Leopard!"

"But you do not have Snake," said Nyame. "So you cannot have my stories."

"Oh no" thought Anansi. "I still have Snake to catch - the deadliest creature of them all! What am I going to do? I am not the strongest or the most fierce and I am not very brave ..." he said to himself.

 "I will just have to use more of my skill, my wit and my cleverness to catch him out!"

Anansi went to fetch a long bamboo pole and some rope.

Then he walked along the road by Snake's home, laughing and talking to himself.

"Longer and stronger or shorter and weaker? Which is it? Which is it?" he said over and over again.

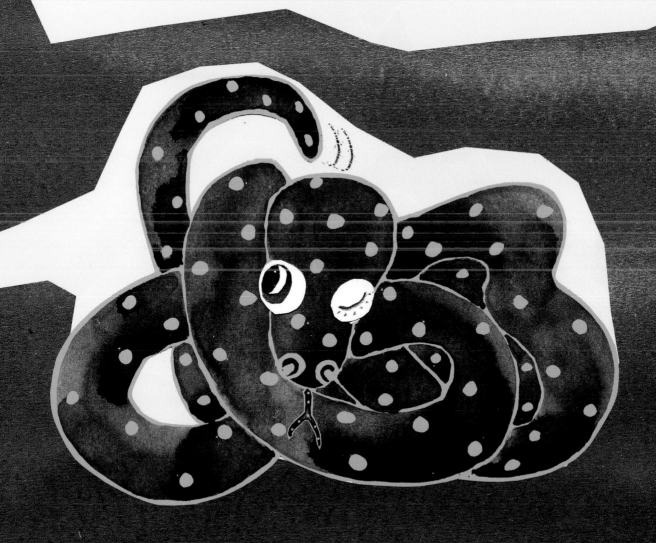

Snake saw Anansi laughing and talking to himself.
"Hey!" called Snake, "What's the matter with you?"

"I am trying to work out whether you are longer and stronger than this bamboo pole or shorter and weaker," said Anansi.

"That's easy, I am longer and stronger." said Snake. "Just put the bamboo pole down on the ground and you will see!"

So Anansi put the bamboo pole down on the ground next to Snake.

"No, I think you are a bit shorter." said Anansi.

Snake was angry. "If I stretch out, you will be able to see how I am longer and stronger," said Snake.

And Snake stretched out.

"The thing is," said Anansi, "when you stretch out, your top half gets longer but your bottom half gets shorter."

"Then tie me to the bamboo pole so that I cannot move," said Snake.

"Good thinking!" said Anansi, smiling to himself.

So Anansi tied Snake
to the bamboo pole so
that he could not move.

"Like I said before, I am longer and stronger than this bamboo pole!" said Snake.

"Oh no, you're not," laughed Anansi. "You are weaker and shorter and very, very foolish!"

Anansi dragged Snake all the way back to Nyame.
"I have him!" Anansi sang. "I have Snake!"
"So you do," said Nyame. "So you do."

"And I must keep my word ..." said Nyame. "From this day on, all stories shall belong to you, and you shall be known as Anansi King of Stories!"

"Now everyone will come and hear about me!" said Anansi.

And that is how Anansi got his stories.

Retell the story

Once upon a time...

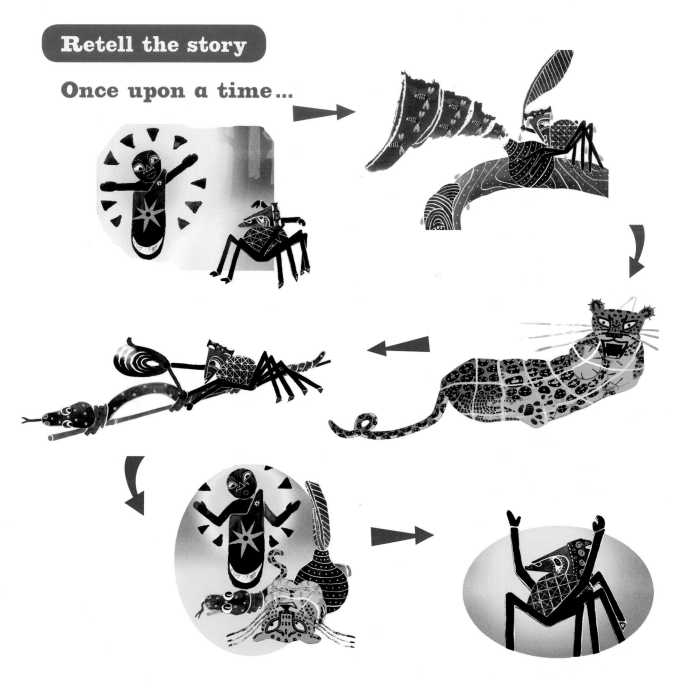

The end.